If, because of me

Memories and Love Poems for Ginny

by Leon Knight

other books by Leon Knight

poetry

SINGING ON THE MOUNTAIN
THE FORTUNATE OF MEN
KNIGHTSONG
SOME WORDS HAVE WINGS
A DISTANT LAND—NEAR poetry by Zhang Yun and Leon Knight

prose

VERA'S RETURN

college texts

THE FIVE STAGES OF WRITING
COLLEGE ENGLISH READER Selections by Leon Knight

International Standard Book Number 0-9635690-8-2
Copyright © 1996 TA Publications

ALL RIGHTS RESERVED

Reproduction in whole or in part without written permission is prohibited, except by a reviewer who may quote brief passages in a review.

Printed in the United States of America

CONTENTS

FORTY YEARS TOGETHER (and still counting) by Leon Knight
"WORK IN PROGRESS" 1
THE RISK OF SPRING 2
FAMILY TREE 2
ALL I HAVE 3
GRANDMOTHER DIED CONTENT 3
IN '39 THE MEN CAME THROUGH 4
THE HOUSE ON THE IOWA FARM 5
LIFE GONE WRONG 6
PITY THE MAN 6
SINCE GRANDMA DIED 7
SHADOWS IN THE NIGHT 7
I FELT MIST EVERYWHERE 8
THE NEW HIGHWAY 8
MOTHER 9
I AGE LIKE THE PINE TREE 9
PEACE COMES SLOWLY 10
AUTUMN COMES 10
WHEN I LOST MY HOME 11
THE BRIDGE OF BONES 12
THE BROTHER 12
WHEN OUR TIME CAME 13
I WONDER WHY 13
THE MOURNING DOVE 14
THOSE DISTANT DAYS 14
ON THE NECESSITY OF RESTRAINT 15
WHEN EVE WAS WRINKLED 15
ON THE PRAIRIE 16
BELIEVE ME I-II-III 17-19
MY GARLAND IN HER HAIR 20
ON OUR JOURNEY HOME 21
WHISPERS OF MY NAME 22
WHEN I HAD DREAMS 23
I WANT YOU WITH ME 24
EVEN AS I PICK THE BUD 24
SOMETHING REAL 25
I PLANTED MY HEART 25
FALL FILLS ME 26
THE LAST WORD 26
THE LOTUS 27
I KNOW WHERE EDEN IS 28
ONCE BEFORE I DIE 28

I WRITE POEMS	29
A QUIET WOMAN	29
IF, BECAUSE OF ME	30
TWO-PART HARMONY	31
THEN GINNY TOUCHED ME	31
SOME WORDS HAVE WINGS	32
WHEN FREEDOM COMES	33
THE SEAWALL	34
DEATH AND DYING	34
I RISE IN OPPOSITION	35
HEAD-GAMES	36
LEAVING HERE	36
OCTOBER MELANCHOLY	37
A DARK JOURNEY	38
ABOUT YOU AND WRITING POEMS	39
THE WIND AND I	39
LOVING YOU	40
AN OLD MAN'S HEART	41
THIS TIME	41
SONG IN THE SOFT RAIN	42
YOU LEFT BY PLANE	42
DO NOT WAKE THE SUN	43
AGAINST THE WIND	43
A STAND OFF	44
FEELING LOW	44
LAUGH ALL YOU WANT	45
YOUR GIFT DIVINE	45
THE FORTUNATE OF MEN	46
SITTING ON THE WIND	46
LOVE ENTERS THIS HOUSE	47
WHEN I AM OLD	47
WALK WITH ME IN MOONLIGHT	48
WE WILL BE TRUE	48
I'D LIKE TO GIVE YOU BUTTERFLIES	49
DRINK THIS CUP WITH ME	49
BUT YESTERDAY	50
YOU ARE BEAUTIFUL	50
AND I WILL TOUCH YOU GENTLY	51
WE MUST TELL THE PEOPLE	51
SINGING ON THE MOUNTAIN	52
I KNOW WHAT IT IS	52
JUST REMEMBER	53

FORTY YEARS TOGETHER
(and still counting)
by Leon Knight

In December of 1955, I was stationed in California at a U.S. Navy base near San Francisco and Ginny was a student at San Jose State. By chance, my home leave began the same day she started her Christmas break. So I arranged to ride with her as she and a roommate drove home to Arizona and I began my hitchhike home to Minnesota.

Although we had met some months earlier, we had not dated before that ride together. Maybe it was just the eight hours together in that car, but I don't think so. (I do not remember anything at all about her roommate who shared that ride.) For whatever reason, that time together before she dropped me off on old Route 66 on the California-Arizona border convinced me of something.

So early in January when I got back from leave, I telephoned her for a date. She said yes. And less than two months later — March 2, 1956 — at a Southern Baptist Church in San Jose, California, in a ceremony officiated by Rev. Harold Dye, Ginny and I were married.

In one sense, our actual wedding was delayed because at that time, since I was under 21 years of age, I had to write home to get my parents' permission to marry. So on that Friday evening — the earliest date we could arrange — we got married. And on Monday morning, I went back to work and she went back to college.

According to the experts, there was not one thing that was right about our marriage. I had no education and no prospects (except the G.I. bill). My navy pay was low, and we could look forward to a number of years of poverty until I completed college after my navy enlistment. We grew up in different parts of the country and had dated a very short time. So we didn't really know each other very well at all. In other words, everything was wrong.

Except . . . everything was right.

(I wonder if Ginny would charge me interest if I were to repay the money I borrowed for the marriage license all those years ago.)

*****

I learned that a marriage will either break under pressure or become stronger when Ginny and I were put through the fire in 1963.

After I completed graduate school at Harvard, I accepted a job as an English teacher at a mission school in what was then called Southern Rhodesia (now Zimbabwe). After about a year in that racist, everything-is-political colony, I was forced to leave the country for siding with my African colleagues and friends in favor of African independence.

About a week before our forced departure, a group of missionary women (all white, of course) wanted to have a good-bye tea for

Ginny. They wanted to let her know that, although they considered me to be completely reprehensible, they liked her — she just had the bad luck of marrying the wrong man. Once she realized what their purpose was, she told them, "You should know that I think my husband is right." Thus, Ginny refused to attend the good-bye tea.

And, thus, our marriage withstood the test of fire — our life together held water. When she could have easily hidden or ducked or said, "You're on your own in this," she stood up and told the world, "I'm with him. I'll leave with the man I came with."

I knew then that, whatever tough times we faced in the future, I would never be alone. And I vowed — neither would she.

* * * * *

In April of 1978, we were planning a second sabbatical to southern Africa. (The first in 1970-71 was combined with a special literature program at the University of London.) During the physical exam in preparation for the trip, Ginny's doctor found something suspicious, kept checking and eventually ordered a bone marrow test.

The diagnosis — leukemia . . . a chronic form that the textbooks say is "uniformly fatal." Now almost eighteen years later, fewer than three percent of those diagnosed about that time are still alive.

Shortly after Ginny was diagnosed, she told me, "I have no idea how much time I have. And I don't want to waste any of it feeling sorry for myself or living with someone who mopes around with a long face all of the time. Regardless of how much time we have together, life is to be lived."

* * * * *

So, you see — I was right back in 1956. (Lucky too, I must admit.)

This book — *IF, BECAUSE OF ME*, memories and love poems written at various times during our years together — is to let the world know what I've tried to show Ginny privately — how much our time together has meant to me.

And I'm still lucky in 1996 — forty years together . . . and still counting! What a way to go!

"WORK IN PROGRESS"
(a love poem)

I lie when I publish
    love poems —
hundreds of them
but, really,
    one would do —
    dozens named
but, really, only one,
    only you.

I've published volumes
    of love poems,
each poem complete,
able to break
    any romantic heart,
but, really,
    my one love poem
is a "work in progress" —
each volume published
just one
    small part.

THE RISK OF SPRING

planting seed's the risk
    of spring,
having faith that fall
    will bring
harvest sufficient
    for the dark,
fruit and flowers
    for the ark.
sailing, sailing on
    winter's sea;
sustained by risk,
    or the cold claims me.

carefully, carefully
we plant the seeds
and do our best
    (we could still get weeds.)

FAMILY TREE

I sometimes walk
    at night
to the park to see
    the golden moon
hanging among branches
of the birch tree.

And I think of my father.

Then I remember:
I too have a family
    tree.

ALL I HAVE

Love   (like life)
must surely end
and, oh, the pain.
But I would gamble
    all I have
and risk such loss
    again.

GRANDMOTHER DIED CONTENT

Grandmother died content —
    her fantasies were small —
the best cabbage
    in the township;
completing the quilt
    before the baby came.

Her furniture was never new.
Her "best" clothes lasted years.
She voted when she could
    but never worried
    about the counting.

The size of her world
didn't extend much beyond
    the rim of her cup,
    smells of her kitchen,
    sounds of grandchildren.

Her fantasies were small —
    she died content.

IN '39 THE MEN CAME THROUGH

In '39 the men came through stringing power poles.
My father put lights in our barn and house
        and a yard light in between.
In the evenings
he'd light the yard an extra time,
and we'd sit on the porch just to watch our light.

Sometimes I'd climb the mill to see how far I'd see,
        picking out the places by their lights.
I'd see Olson's and Tourney's, the Swancutt place
and Brown's.   Even Grandpa's three miles away.
        If I looked north,
I could see the light on the water tank in town.

When mother called, "Son, come down for bed,"
I answered,   "Hey, Mom, can you see the lights?
        I can see all the way to Grandpa's!"
        * * * * *
        Oh, it was a glorious time,
        a golden time,
        a sighting-from-the-windmill time,
        that summer of '39.
        * * * * *

I'd climb the platform of our mill,
or lie flat atop our little hill
        and cup my hands,
cutting out the earth-bound green,
        to gaze skyward
at the soft underbelly of hanging clouds.
Soft gray surrounded by glaring white
and endless blue.
        And I'd wonder
how soft and white it must be above those clouds.

The summer sun soothed my skin as I lay there,
        my warmed blood flowing out
between ripples, like the stream below,
        to form the stills and pools.

From time to time a plane would pass,
though ours was a seldom farm,
      and my cupped hands became a scope
      to spy on other worlds — wondering
where that plane was bound and what the pilot knew.
      * * * * *
Later, I'd run across the slough, laughing
among the turkey grass, the cattails and the reeds.
      Ever running —
for stopping meant I'd fill a boot
and mother got so mad —
until I got to solid ground where I could stop
and watch killdeer walking funny in the sand.

THE HOUSE ON THE IOWA FARM

The house on the Iowa farm
was torn down for lumber.
The farmer, with Rural Free Delivery,
now has a number
for a third-floor, walk-up flat —
shrivelled up and useless now
like some forgotten apple
on an awkward bough.

LIFE GONE WRONG

Bitter feelings at times engulf me:
life doesn't sail as I foresaw;
freezing winds keep on rising,
not as breezes but blowing raw.

So I've learned to hunker down,
to bend my back before life's gale;
but even as I yearn for haven,
I hear the song within the wail.

The rising wind carries menace,
piercing notes of the driven song;
but I thank God there is the music,
poems to write about life gone wrong.

PITY THE MAN

I pitied the man who wept
    from a broken heart
because a loved one died
till
    I met a man without a heart
    who never, ever cried.

SINCE GRANDMA DIED

A big, home-cooked meal
is not that big a deal
    — no more.

SHADOWS IN THE NIGHT

Light of moon and sparkling stars
    is caught by ghosts
and memories   forming
    shadows in the night —
shadows that flicker
    past moist eyelids —
shadows that mock
    the golden light.

The shadows lead
    through dark recesses
    down hard-walked roads
    to the cold tombstone
where grief combines with shadows
    to teach us —
each walks that last hard-road alone.

We learn from shadows
that mock   and lead us
on life's great trek
    to the final rite.
The death of loved ones
    is our sunset —
thus, we can see
    shadows in the night.

I FELT MIST EVERYWHERE
(for Grandma)

When she died,
      I felt —
well, not exactly pain,
      though resembling it
      as mist resembles rain.
A thin film of it
      covering everything,
making colors deeper, more alive;
      not blinding me —
filling my eyes with driven rain;
but seeing more clearly,
      my senses revived.

When she died,
      I felt mist everywhere,
putting off work I had to complete,
feeling cold or sticky warm,
      ignoring victory,
      forgetting defeat.

THE NEW HIGHWAY

In high school
      I was lucky —
a new highway was built
17 miles east of town.

      Leaving was easy.

MOTHER

Mother,
    in pain and love,
gave life;
    in hope and confusion,
developed life;
    with fear and courage,
defended life —
all the while unaware,
    dear brother,
preparing us for this:
we'll be the next to die.

I AGE LIKE THE PINE TREE

I age like the pine tree —
    evergreen
and ever changing.
Recording life in rings,
powerless rings of memories
    sucked in
through roots and limbs.
Marking sun and cold
and rain in aging lines,
    permanent,
        clear and deep.

PEACE COMES SLOWLY

Peace comes slowly
Dripping from my bones
Like honey from a honeycomb
That took ages of bees to fill.
The comb built right
From the belly of the bees
Who could feel,
Somewhere off
In the winter of the hive,
A coming cry
For honey.
And the honey finally flows,
After the bees,
Drop by drop,
Have filled the empty comb.

AUTUMN COMES

I sometimes forget
      why
I live in Minnesota —
      autumn comes.
Then I remember.

WHEN I LOST MY HOME

When I lost
    my home, the world
opened up for me.
The house where I was born
    was torn apart
    for lumber,
        and I moved on.

    The only place
where I was never lonely
    is gone for me
        forever.
The lonely call
    of the loon
gave way   to cactus wren.
And the sight of white-
    tailed deer
blends with kudu
on this valley's other side.

For lunch with my grandbabies,
we share   idobi
    in taco shells
and drink Darjeeling tea.

THE BRIDGE OF BONES

How many bones
to build a bridge
to cross the sea?
      How many
shark-feed souls?

Their spirits should rise
up   a mighty light —
      a light so clear,
      a light so bright —
we finally see
      the bridge of bones —
ancestors' bones across the sea
connecting
      me to you
and   you to me.

THE BROTHER
(for Obadiah)

When I was young upon the Iowa fields
As ten-year drought was drying up the birch
And causing breaking of the family farm
That sent me hungry on a brother search,
You ran across the slopes of southern hills
And with a mission sought for something new.
But learning often causes family splits —
Leaving separate me and lonely you.
It's not within the womb that brothers meet.
They meet upon the green of grazing field,
Or first touch hands and hearts in Harvard Yard,
Or join the battle behind a common shield.
But wherever met, life is made complete
When, at last, true brothers finally meet.

WHEN OUR TIME CAME
(for Godfrey and Vengai)

When we were young
we stood side by side.
You put your livelihood
 and even your life
on the line
to stand with me
 when our time came.

Our time —
 not of our choosing —
came up as the dawn,
and we stood in the bright glare
 facing the sun
  together.
And now
we can rest in the shade
because we know —
 when our time came —
we stood together,
 each earning the right
 when we were young
to be called
 a man.

I WONDER WHY

I wonder why
 I wonder why
when I know
 I'll never know
  why
tiny drops of anguish
 erode the soul
as rainfall marks the mountain
 stone,
moving sand down to the sea —
 going home,
  going home.

THE MOURNING DOVE

Oh, mourning dove, singing
to me from the roadside,
    cry on.
Sweet mother, cry on.
Grandmother, who sang my father's farm
and sang me laughing on my way,
now you're laughing, as you cry,
that I can't hear your song;
the song that soothed grandfather's ears,
the song that lifted father's eyes —
    the song I cannot hear.
My car's too loud as I race the road,
raising dust to hide your nest,
raising noise to hide your song,
not hearing you as you cry.
    Sad mother, cry on.
Grandmother,
    as I disappear in dust,
        cry on.

THOSE DISTANT DAYS
(before Hiroshima)

Let's not talk of distant days
When dead men marched to glory,
When school girls sought to sing their praise,
And young men knew . . .

Those distant days are dead.

ON THE NECESSITY OF RESTRAINT

Everything goes
when "anything goes."

WHEN EVE WAS WRINKLED

When Eve was wrinkled
(and Adam old),
she sat one evening with her man
to watch the stars unfold.
Her great grandchildren
and other little ones
were in their first sleep,
so the camp was quiet,
      except the rustling of restless sheep.
The old woman,
      for the first time in years,
thought of Cain
and of Abel
(she loved them both — the slayer and the slain)
and Seth (the good one)
      who gave her grandbabies.
As Adam emptied ashes in the sand,
Eve said,
      "We've had the damnedest time, haven't we?"
Even in the dark she knew he smiled
as he pressed her hand:
      "You're right about that, old girl.
      If we could do it again, do you think we should?"
Leaning back to see the moon, she sighed:
      "Oh, my dear — if we only could."

ON THE PRAIRIE

On the prairie
stands a lonely tree
    silhouetted
against the sky,
    shaped by ancient,
    relentless wind.
As I got close,
    I found wildflowers
    amidst the grass
    around the tree,
too close
    for the farmer's plow.

(I didn't need the tree
    to think of you —
lately, I believe
    I think of little else.)

The tree was alone
    and surviving,
    bent slightly,
    withstanding years,
sheltering flowers and prairie grass,
offering peaceful shade
    to the traveler.

Beneath the tree,
    I thought again of you
    and wished (forlornly)
I could enjoy your shadow forever.

BELIEVE ME: I

If I seem mad,
Believe me.
Death was one thing
For grandpa,
For he was old;
Or for Sam,
For there was war.
But she's not old.
She's not in war.
All
There is is
Death.
He's come to take her,
My one, best friend.
That slimy ooze
Has come to take her.
I beat my chest.
I tear my hair.
I shake my fists.
And still that putrid corruption
Comes to take her.
I scream.
I fight.
I kick.
And I can't stop him.
So if I seem mad,
Believe me.

BELIEVE ME: II

If I seem sad,
Believe me.
As I watch the full moon
Disappear
Behind cold clouds,
The huddled earth
Is dark, and October
Rain names
The coming of the cold,
The long cold
Hushing earth
To memories,
Memories to fill
Lost and lonely spaces.
Memories of water birds
Before the river froze.
Memories of sun
Sets when the sun would
Rise again.
Already I know
What lonely is.
So if I seem sad,
Believe me.

BELIEVE ME: III

If I seem glad,
Believe me.
If I know what I'm losing,
I know what I've got:
I've got a song
To sing.
It was taught to me
By a rainbow
Before the rainbow disappeared.
And I learned to sing
By heart:
Two-part
Harmony, soul
Music with the rhythm of blood
And the beat of my heart.
And did we dance!
For over 40 years,
With each step new.
Our own song:
We made the words,
We made the tune,
We danced the dance.
Yes, because of her,
I've got a song to sing.
So if I seem glad,
Believe me.

MY GARLAND IN HER HAIR

In the twilight
    I remember
the morning sun
       leaping from her hiding place
       and running across the veldt.
She laughed and teased,
    enticing me
    to chase her.
         Youthful lover,
    I ran my heedless way.
But she was wise
    (and cunning)
         beyond my knowing.
She catered to my ego:
she danced with joy
    when I found wildflowers
    no one else could see.
She even wore my garland in her hair.
And I knew   (I knew)
      she had never known another
        quite like me.

Now as I sit here
        in the twilight
as the sun drops quickly from the sky,
I regret — I love
and I am grateful
that she led me to wildflowers,
that someone wore my garland
       before I died.

ON OUR JOURNEY HOME

On our journey home, my love,
we're travelling slow
      with nothing
but our lives of time.

We stop at different places,
      places few men ever go —
we eat strange food,
we see strange sights,
we love strange loves
      and learn to live
with illusion and disillusion
      on our journey home.

Strange smells now waft our room.
Strange scenes now mural our walls.
Strange loves now live our lives,
      and people with big eyes
      walk quickly down our street.

Behind the curtain, I weep
as I watch their shadows scurry by.
      I weep
not for our loneliness but theirs
and those illusions lost
amid the smells, the sights, the sounds
      on our journey home.

WHISPERS OF MY NAME

I turn to see my steps trail
      lonely on the beach,
the gulls searching
the ebb and tidal pools.
I find the cave still damp
and fondle the abandoned conch —
rounded, smooth and cool —
given me by the sea.
      I listen
to hear it speak your name,
but it whispers mine . . .
as I stretch on damp sand
warmed quickly by the sun.
      I listen again
      to hear your name,
but the shell, more clearly now,
again calls me.
      And I know your voice —
      you call to me.
As I follow the siren sound
into the cave, we meet
in whispered love, in aching arms,
      in trembling touch . . .
as sea shells shout my name.
      When I awaken,
the cave is warm, the sand is dry,
the conch still smooth and cool.
Carefully, I carry it home where,
      watching sunsets,
I hold it close
      to hear your voice
      and whispers of my name.

WHEN I HAD DREAMS

I remember
        when I had dreams —
        big dreams,
               small dreams,
        medium dreams.
I had a thousand,
               thousand dreams.

Oh, that was a time —
I could move then,
        and the whole world
moved   with me.
I even had a lady
        who loved me,
me —   the real rebellious me!
        She loved me!
Ah, when life was like that,
I couldn't do
        nothing wrong
               — nothing

Yeah,   I had dreams —
        a thousand,
               thousand dreams.

I WANT YOU WITH ME

I want you with me
      as I'm dying,
demanding everything of love
till there's nothing else to give,
wanting the warmth, the joy, the pain
till there's nothing else to live.

Or, I'll be with you
      as you're dying,
feeling that last measure of joy
      of a broken heart
made full as we live,
made pure as we part.

EVEN AS I PICK THE BUD

Even as I pick the bud,
I feel the fade of roses.
So soon,
With the bud still in my hand,
Still here to touch,
My memory,
Before it becomes memory,
Must fill the vacant spaces
With the lost
Scent of roses.

SOMETHING REAL

When I was young,
    I really thought
        the sun came up
           with me,
        the radio was silent
           till I turned it on,
    I would surely
        change the world.

Of course, childish fantasies
had to submit
    to something real —
by luck,
    to something infinitely
        more wonderful,
        more pleasurable,
        more true.
The sun doesn't rise with me;
I haven't changed the world;
but
    I have meant something
        good
        to you.

I PLANTED MY HEART

I planted my heart
    in you,
and   I grew
like saguaro
    on the dry plain.
What would I do
    with someone else
who would send me
    too much rain?

FALL FILLS ME

Fall fills me
      with molten gold,
then adds silver,
      reds and browns
to make my heart explode,
Such spring-completing color
summer's pledge fulfilled,
makes me forget
      — and then accept —
the coming winter's chill.

THE LAST WORD
(for Ginny)

when   all   is summarized
                          for me
          you
will be   the last word

THE LOTUS
(for Ginny,
who grew up in Arizona)

The lotus rises from useless mud
but is pure in every part —
      the root an edible tuber,
      the nut a delicate heart.

The leaf is used for cooking rice.
The colorful flower
      has a soothing face.
The lotus —
      a beautiful symbol
of someone low achieving grace.

No wonder the Buddha chose
      the lotus
      for his throne.

* * * * * * *

But it is a wonder
      the lotus would choose
      the desert for her home.

I KNOW WHERE EDEN IS

I know where Eden is:
> in the mountains by the sea,
> soothed by the pungent scent
> of eucalyptus trees.

Near the cliff cavort the whales
> blowing plumes of spray;
they roll to show their flukes
> and slap their tails in play.

I know what Adam felt
> in Eden near the sea:
Eve was there with him,
> and you were there with me.

ONCE BEFORE I DIE
(for Morgan)

Once before I die,
I'd like to hear an eagle cry
As it swoops in not forgotten flight
Across the empty sky.
The sky where crows grow silent
While chickens run to hide.
For until the eagle passes,
All else has partly died.
The eyes don't raise for chickens.
Cawing crows don't make a dream.
So once before I die,
Let me hear the eagle scream.

I WRITE POEMS

I have no money,
I'm not 'Big Daddy'
And I write poems:
That makes me
      a tough love,
And you . . .
      a very special lady.

A QUIET WOMAN

I live with a quiet woman.
(Note that —   I   live
      with a quiet woman.)

She's eliminated fat
      from talk,   chewing
      high protein close to bone,
a life-long diet
      leaving her soul
      lean   and   clean
      hard bodied,
capable
      of silences
      and empty places,
unafraid
      of quiet and space,
unthreatened
      by my silent place.

I live   with
      a quiet woman.

IF, BECAUSE OF ME

If, because of me, you think
    you're beautiful,
it's because . . . you are beautiful.
If, because of me, you think
    you're desirable,
it's because . . . you are desired.
If, because of me, you think
    you've touched the wind,
    and felt the rain
and made a place of private heart,
it's because we did . . .
    touch the wind,
    and feel the rain
    and make a private place
        of heart.
And if, because of me, you feel
we once again are young.
    Well, we're not young,
    but we have caught
        and held the sun.

TWO-PART HARMONY

We merged
my seldom song
with your private tune,
and we sang
our new song
over and over again
until,
        to our delight,
        we now know it
        by heart.

THEN GINNY TOUCHED ME

I used to think
a woman's hands were weak.
        Then Ginny touched me —
        I got all tied in knots.

SOME WORDS HAVE WINGS

Some words have wings
and move delicately
      through the air
like monarch butterflies
      — catching light
      and sparkling —
words like   "honor"
      "duty" "loyalty"
Words on great migrations —
squashed against the windshield
or pinned upon the wall —
buffeted by hot wind
      but always moving
towards the shimmering, southern tree.
The holy grove where monarchs swarm
      holds promises
      brighter and more wonderful
than any tree loaded
      with Christmas lights
      and pious decorations.

Some words are silent
      like the wings of an owl.
"Freedom" is heard so often
      you think you know
          what freedom is.
Then late one night —
      with huge eyes seeing
      hidden, secret things —
it comes   — unbidden,
      unwelcome, silent —
to sink its claws into your gut.
And you become consumed.

Some words have wings
      like the bumblebee.
They are forced to carry
      more weight
than they seem able to bear.
A word like   "Love."
      Isn't it wonderful
      that the bumblebee flies?

WHEN FREEDOM COMES
(for Martin Luther King, Jr.)

When freedom comes,
As it must surely come,
Like the stream of light in the east
Announcing the wayward sun
Or like a flash of lightning
Reminding us that even storms,
Fearful in the night, bring rain
By which the earth's reborn —
When it finally comes —
This freedom,
This life,
This urgent, needful thing —
When it, at last, arrives,
We'll think of you, racked martyr,
And see you in the lives
Of children dancing
To music we only dreamed before,
And we'll see you in the eyes
Of widows sharing communion bread
Grown from soil grown rich
With the blood of our enduring dead.
Then in our daily dance
And in our daily bread,
We'll honor you
With this hard and heart-felt pledge:
What's been won by you and countless
Courageous women and heroic men
Will never — never — never
Be stolen from us again.

THE SEAWALL

I sometimes get feeling weary —
    nothing special,
    just life wore down.
Beachcombing was never for me —
    no lazy sailing,
    no seaweed crown.

With resolve, I try to stand here —
    my loved ones' seawall
    before life's tide.
I know I must just stand here —
    though at times I'm weary
    and I weep inside.

DEATH AND DYING
(for Lee)

A friend said
he could accept death
but dying got him down.

I know what he means —
    it's the difference
    between a noun
    and a verb.
Dying is a verb,
    so is living
    and loving —
not like death at all.

I RISE IN OPPOSITION

I rise in opposition
To the motion,
The inevitable motion,
Of the Minister of State.
I know, in the minority,
The Honorable State has power
To determine final form.

Still I must rise
Like the kite against the wind.
The wind is blowing north;
The kite is anchored south,
Not to defeat the wind
(Martyrdom's not my goal)
But to soar to the top of it.
When people see a kite
They know the wind
Is not just
For turning mills
Or pushing sails.
And, oh, if they knew
What the kite knows
About surrender to the wind —

No sir! I will not yield
I've risen in opposition.

HEAD-GAMES

The teacher lectures
on "The Bill of Rights" —
      students comb their hair.

LEAVING HERE

I am leaving here —
these concrete walls
shall hear my call
      no more.
My unheard voice
      of warning
shall still
in mountain morning,
      somewhere
west and north of Santa Fe.
My tired, aching flesh
will once again be blessed
      as I rejoice
the drawing down of day.

OCTOBER MELANCHOLY

October — melancholy
    in the rain,
    colors muted,
    leaves limp —
not whirling
in the dance
of children
    playing, unaware
    of autumn's fall
    to earth.
I feel the ache
    of summers past —
youthful hero learning
to "play with pain"

This gray, damp afternoon,
    low, dark clouds
    move in
to hold my spirit down —
making me more aware
    that pain hurts —
the right time
for private time
with a warm friend,
    if one be found.

A DARK JOURNEY
(for Ginny)

Mine was a dark journey.
Like the wise men
Coming from the east,
I saw the stars.
(Cold nights
And camel smells)

And frightened shepherds —
(Sheep are dumb,
Dumber than camels,
Though not as mean.)

But this journey has nothing
To do with camels and sheep.
It has to do with following stars —
First, with seeing them,
With being able to live
In the dark and see
The stars.
With being my own
Astronomer,
My own astrologer.
(And the shimmering moon
On ice-blue lake)
And, finally,
With watching the sun
And the moon
Till I looked up,
Unafraid,
To see
The evening star.

ABOUT YOU AND WRITING POEMS
(for Ginny)

I want you near
       — please forgive me —
as I drop into myself
searching for the perfect pearl
or lost treasure
or the beauty
       of the underwater world.

Leaving earth and easy air,
I go down
       (sometimes too deep)
cutting off the ordinary light
and the world of sound.

It's like first water in a mother's womb —
       the eyes gain sight,
       the head grows clear.
But coming back to earth, my lungs hurt.
So,   please forgive me,
       but I need you near.

THE WIND AND I

I sit
on the side of a mountain
looking at a hundred
spires shaped by the wind
and feel the evening
breeze singing
in the piñon trees.
I feel it,
and it feels good.

But I leave no mark
on the wind.

LOVING YOU
(for those who love me)

You have
        a face I'm always glad
                to look upon;
you are someone
        I'm always glad I'm near;
you   renew my soul,
        refresh my heart,
and help remove the fear
I've had
        of that fate-filled, final part.
I've asked, "What's life about?"
and,   because of you,
        I now can shout,
                "I know! I've learned!
                I'm infant-wise!"
and able (now — at last)
        to see beyond the lies,
lies wiped away by you — your touch,
your presence, your gentle style.
        Being loved by you
                and loving you
        has   — to my wonder —
        made life
                worthwhile.

AN OLD MAN'S HEART

The bull giraffe
        battle scarred
        and weary
alone
        dark colored —
        shadowed
like the covering
of an old man's heart
        silent — no wisdom
        to pass on —
        unable to speak
like so many of us
            men
        when we get old

THIS TIME

I wish we would never
        have to say good-bye.
I wish
I would never feel
        the need to cry
as   I watch long shadows
        in the fast-falling sun
reminding me,
        even as we feast,
this time   together
        is nearly done.
Please dance with me
        this (final) time,
and I will claim forever
this time   as mine.

SONG IN THE SOFT RAIN

It is raining
      a soft rain,
    so gentle
colors of flowers
      come more alive,
birds sing more sweetly
and my friend walks with me
      laughing
          under my umbrella.

YOU LEFT BY PLANE

I wish you had left
      by sailing ship
so I, like land-bound Columbus,
could watch my yearnings fade
      over the horizon
      out to sea.

Instead, you left by plane.
In one short minute,
      a distant glint.
Then endless, empty sky
staring back at me.

DO NOT WAKE THE SUN

Do not wake the sun,
for then,
       in the unforgiving west,
       the light shall surely fade,
while the sun's faint hope
       is forever
       in the east.

She was born
       east of the sun.
But   to love me,
       she awakened
       in the west.
And now she fades.

       Oh, to slow that sun!

AGAINST THE WIND

All sand once was rock.
       Water and wind —
even when I'm silent,
I am ground to dust.

I struggle
       against the current —
downstream lies the swamp.

When I die
       (if you love me)
throw my ashes
       against the wind.

A STAND OFF
(Survivor's Creed)

The world is not perfect;
        neither am I:
we've worked out
        an accommodation.

FEELING LOW

I sometimes believe
God has terminated the investment
        in a failed experiment,
    written humans off
        as an unproven hypothesis —
a good idea
        that just didn't work out.

When I feel that low,
I really don't know
    what I'd do
        without you.

LAUGH ALL YOU WANT

Laugh all you want
at my beard full of gray —
    Ginny loves me
    just this way.

YOUR GIFT DIVINE
(for Ginny)

When I was young,
I wanted to give you all
    the universe.
But now,
    as I grow old,
you have given me
    the earth.

Even here,
    in far away Zimbabwe
with you at our midwestern home,
I feel life more keenly
and see with eyes grown
    clear by life-long love,
the mystery of your gift divine,
that has (God be praised!)
    made earth mine.

THE FORTUNATE OF MEN

When I think of what I was
When first we met,
Or think about what might have been
I look at you and know
I am the fortunate of men.

For what I am and what you are
We built together.
The bow's the moment of the sun and rain.
And heaven is ticked around the stars.
The moment lost can never be regained.

My gain is you — my moment you,
So whatever else is to be done,
Already you've given me the moon
Together we've caught and held the sun.

I am the fortunate of men.

SITTING ON THE WIND

I like
Sitting on the wind,
Like a gull
Or an eagle.
Facing into it
And spreading my wings.

LOVE ENTERS THIS HOUSE

Love, bearing new life,
        enters this house
comes as to her own home,
comes to give a feast.
There she is, hovering over
        these her children.

Love, bearing new life,
        flies through this house
all the rooms she sweeps
the wings of love sweep clean
making clear this place
        sweeping out
        the harm and danger.

WHEN I AM OLD

When I am old
And sitting in the sun
Watching as tide-bound waves
Wash away sand castles
Built one by one
By playing children,
I shall think of you
And watch as fading castles
Melt in foam-flecked waves
That lift my eyes
And still warm heart
To misty, billowing clouds
And in those clouds
I'll see your face
And somewhere, you will know
As soft white clouds merge
And dance across the sky,
Someone does love
The gentle soul of you.

WALK WITH ME IN MOONLIGHT

Come, walk with me
    in moonlight.
We'll rejoice the close of day.
    Talk with me
as moonlight sparkles dreams
    before our way.

Draw closer in the moonlight;
feel warmth within my arms —
drink deep the cup of moonlight;
drink deep the magic charms.

We'll learn poetry
    by moonlight
(Hold back the falling moon).
We'll drink every drop
    of moonlight,
knowing the sun
    shall rise
        too soon.

WE WILL BE TRUE

Love, we will be true to one another,

    For you are beautiful,
    In a world of little beauty

    You touched me gently
    In a world of violent hurt

    You filled my cup
    In a world that's drinking blood

    You gave me peace
    In a world that knows no peace

Yes, we will be true to one another.

I'D LIKE TO GIVE YOU BUTTERFLIES

I'd like to give you butterflies —
      blues and browns
      and golden swirls,
any color
      your heart beats faster to,
colors to wrap you in —
      a magic comforter,
a quilt of living threads.

I'd like to give you desert blooms —
      flowers surrounded
      by loving thorns,
survivors   — red and yellow —
responding
      to occasional, passionate rain,
finding life   in struggling soil.

Flowers and butterflies —
      and singing birds
(I'd like to give you many things)
the sound of water
      rustling over rocks
and rain drops
      dripping from our eaves.

DRINK THIS CUP WITH ME

Come drink this cup
With me.

Love cures nothing,
But this time
We surely know
Nothing else.

BUT YESTERDAY

But yesterday
      I chased the sun
through showers to find
the rainbow's pot-of-gold.

But yesterday
      I found my love.
(When did I grow old?)

YOU ARE BEAUTIFUL
(to Ginny)

You are beautiful,
      more beautiful than when
      we first joined together
(for now I know more surely
what beauty is).
      Have I been happy?
I no longer think of that
because I've learned
      (with you)
not to be content
with mere happiness —
      we have the sun
      and moon-dance,
      and ten thousand stars.

AND I WILL TOUCH YOU GENTLY

As moonbeams caressed
The sparkling dew
And west wind passed the stars,
As wild geese whistled
Heaven,
And the old man smiled at Mars,
We dance across the water,
Felt shimmering in our hands,
And rose above the earth-line
As if our flight were planned.

And I will touch you gently

Yes, I will touch you gently,
For I have touched the trembling dove,
Learned zephyrs hold no harm.
For I have known fragility,
Held moonglow in my arms.

WE MUST TELL THE PEOPLE

The morning star is on my forehead
The rising sun is in your face
       We must tell the people.

SINGING ON THE MOUNTAIN

We will sing of beauty
Upon the shining mountain.

We will sing the stars
As they trail the western moon.

We will sing the owl
As it gives a voice to night.

We will sing the wind
As it murmurs in the aspen.

We will sing upon the mountain
And our song will touch the sky.

I KNOW WHAT IT IS

I know what it is
    To not fly
        For I have flown
        And been flown;
What it is
    To not dance
        For I have danced
        And been danced;
What it is
    To not sing
        For I have sung
        And been sung;
I know what it is
    To not live
        For I have lived
        And been loved.

JUST REMEMBER

When you are gray, if life grows lonely
and you wonder why nights are cold,
    just remember
    I did love you —
among night shadows, I had you to hold.

Caresses of too-soon spent flesh
made life's sorrow a distant thing;
    just remember
    you did love me —
together we made Eden sing.

Alone, the echo of our song may fade,
but memory can make each day new;
    just remember
    we loved each other —
and our love rang our time true.

NORMANDALE COMMUNITY COLLEGE
LIBRARY
9700 FRANCE AVENUE SOUTH
BLOOMINGTON, MN 55431-4399